Super Dog

BY MICHÈLE DUFRESNE

Pioneer Valley Educational Press, Inc.

"Look at my cape,"
said Jack.
"Look at me
in my red cape!"

Daisy looked at Jack
in his red cape.
"I like your red cape.
Can I wear it?"
she asked.

"No!" said Jack.
"It's **my** red cape.
I'm Super Dog."

S

"Oh!" said Daisy.

"Can you fly?

Can you fly, Super Dog?"

"Yes, I can fly!
I'm going to fly away
in my red cape," said Jack.

S

"You are not flying," said Daisy.

"It's time for lunch," said Jack. "I will fly away **after** lunch."